SIX LITTLE DUCKS

SIX LITTLE DUCKS

Retold and illustrated
by Chris Conover

Thomas Y. Crowell Company
New York

Library of Congress Cataloging in Publication Data

Conover, Chris. Six little ducks. SUMMARY: A retelling
of the nursery song about the six little ducks who go to
market with a quack, quack, quack.
  [1. Songs]   I. Title.
PZ8.3.C7657Si   [784.6] [E]   75-22155
ISBN 0-690-01036-2   ISBN 0-690-01037-0 lib. bdg.

1 2 3 4 5 6 7 8 9 10

Six little ducks that I once knew,
Fat ones, skinny ones, there were too,
But the one little duck
with the feather in his back

He led the others with a

Quack, Quack, Quack.

They started for market one fine day
But lost their wares along the way.

Not a penny in their pocket,
not a nickel in their sack,
They went to the baker with a
Quack, Quack, Quack.

They boldly asked him for some bread,
He shouted back,

So the brave little duck
with the feather in his back
Said "We'll bake our own," with a
Quack, Quack, Quack!

Then the little ducks ate and ate,

Sang and danced

and stayed out late,

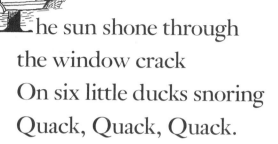

The sun shone through
the window crack
On six little ducks snoring
Quack, Quack, Quack.

One little duck sat up in bed.
He rubbed his eyes and scratched his head.
He looked at the others,
still snug in the sack,
And woke those lazy ducks with a

led the oth-ers with a Quack, Quack, Quack.

CHORUS

Quack, Quack, Quack.

Quack, Quack, Quack, He led the oth-ers with a Quack, Quack, Quack.

They started for market one fine day
But lost their wares along the way.
Not a penny in their pocket,
not a nickel in their sack,
They went to the baker with a
Quack, Quack, Quack.

They boldly asked him for some bread,
He shouted back,
"I'll have your head."
So the brave little duck
with the feather in his back
Said "We'll bake our own," with a
Quack, Quack, Quack!

Then the little ducks ate and ate,
Sang and danced and stayed out late,
The sun shone through
the window crack
On six little ducks snoring
Quack, Quack, Quack.

One little duck sat up in bed.
He rubbed his eyes and scratched his head.
He looked at the others,
still snug in the sack,
And woke those lazy ducks with a
Quack, Quack, Quack!

Chris Conover

A native New Yorker, Chris Conover studied at the High School of
Music and Art and received her B.A.
at the State University of New York
at Buffalo.

She now lives in New York City
where she shares her apartment with
two cats. In the past her pets have
included dogs, rabbits, guinea pigs,
lizards, fish, and birds, many of
whom have made appearances in her
illustrations.

with love and thanks to Sandra

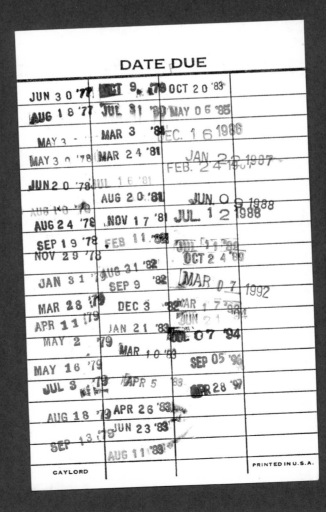